AMAZING SIGHTS IN THE SKY

SHOOTING STARS

by Jane P. Gardner

Ideas for Parents and Teachers

Pogo Books let children practice reading informational text while introducing them to nonfiction features such as headings, labels, sidebars, maps, and diagrams, as well as a table of contents, glossary, and index.

Carefully leveled text with a strong photo match offers early fluent readers the support they need to succeed.

Before Reading

- "Walk" through the book and point out the various nonfiction features. Ask the student what purpose each feature serves.
- Look at the glossary together. Read and discuss the words.

Read the Book

- Have the child read the book independently.
- Invite him or her to list questions that arise from reading.

After Reading

- Discuss the child's questions. Talk about how he or she might find answers to those questions.
- Prompt the child to think more. Ask: Have you ever seen shooting stars? What more do you want to learn about them after reading this book?

Pogo Books are published by Jump!
5357 Penn Avenue South
Minneapolis, MN 55419
www.jumplibrary.com

Library of Congress Cataloging-in-Publication Data

Names: Gardner, Jane P., author.
Title: Shooting stars / by Jane P. Gardner.
Description: Pogo books.
Minneapolis, MN: Jump!, Inc., [2021]
Series: Amazing sights in the sky | Includes index.
Audience: Ages 7-10 | Audience: Grades 2-3
Identifiers: LCCN 2020005989 (print)
LCCN 2020005990 (ebook)
ISBN 9781645275718 (hardcover)
ISBN 9781645275725 (paperback)
ISBN 9781645275732 (ebook)
Subjects: LCSH: Meteors—Juvenile literature. .
Outer space—Juvenile literature.
Reading (Primary)—Juvenile literature.
Classification: LCC QB741.5 .G37 202 (print)
LCC QB741.5 (ebook) | DDC 523.5/1—dc23
LC record available at https://lccn.loc.gov/2020005989
LC ebook record available at https://lccn.loc.gov/2020005990

Editor: Jenna Gleisner
Designer: Molly Ballanger

Photo Credits: sripfoto/Shutterstock, cover; Yuriy Kulik/Shutterstock, 1; Talaj/iStock, 3; Chumphon Whangchom/EyeEm/Getty, 4-5; Mode-list/iStock, 6-7; AlexeyBorodin/iStock, 8-9; Cherdchai charasri/Shutterstock, 10 (top); Torsak Thammachote/Shutterstock, 10 (bottom); guvendemir/iStock, 11; Marko Aliaksandr/Shutterstock, 12-13; Belish/Shutterstock, 14-15; Makarov Konstantin/Shutterstock, 16-17; bjdlzx/iStock, 18-19; Allexxandar/Shutterstock, 20-21; Bjoern Wylezich/Shutterstock, 23.

Printed in the United States of America at Corporate Graphics in North Mankato, Minnesota.

TABLE OF CONTENTS

CHAPTER 1

STREAKS OF LIGHT

Zoom! Streaks of light flash across the night sky. What are they? We call them shooting stars.

meteor

But they're not stars at all. They are **meteors**. These chunks of rock hurl from space. They enter Earth's **atmosphere** and burn up.

Despite its name, space isn't empty. It is filled with rocks and dust grains. They all fly around. These are called **meteoroids**.

When meteoroids enter Earth's atmosphere, they are called meteors. Most meteors burn up and fall. We see shooting stars!

meteoroid

TAKE A LOOK!

Some meteors do not burn up. They make it to Earth's surface. We call them **meteorites**. Take a look!

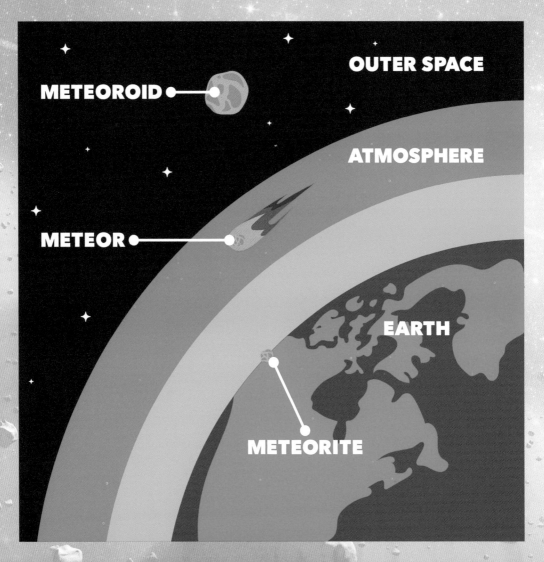

OUTER SPACE

METEOROID

ATMOSPHERE

METEOR

EARTH

METEORITE

Most meteors are very small. **Particles** the size of sand grains form them. Others are larger, maybe the size of basketballs. Some are the size of small cars! When a big, very bright meteor enters our atmosphere, it is called a fireball.

DID YOU KNOW?

Fireballs can be brighter than planets. They burn longer than smaller meteors.

fireball

CHAPTER 2

·····································

THE SCIENCE BEHIND SHOOTING STARS

How do meteors enter Earth's atmosphere? **Gravity**. It pulls all objects toward Earth.

Meteors are very fast. They can travel at speeds of 160,000 miles (257,000 kilometers) per hour! It would take less than two hours to get to the moon from Earth at that speed!

The fast-moving meteors meet with gases in Earth's upper atmosphere. The gases slow them down. This creates **friction**. It also creates heat. The meteors begin to burn. We see shooting stars!

DID YOU KNOW?

How hot are meteors? They burn at temperatures around 3,000 degrees Fahrenheit (1,650 degrees Celsius)! That is hot enough to melt iron!

Shooting stars appear white. But photographs of them tell a more colorful story. Red, yellow, purple, orange, and teal are just some of the colors. Their makeup determines the colors we see.

TAKE A LOOK!

A meteor's **elements** give it its color. Take a look!

NITROGEN OR OXYGEN

MAGNESIUM

IRON

CALCIUM

SODIUM

CHAPTER 3

METEOR SHOWERS

Every August, the **Northern Hemisphere** gets a show. As many as 100 meteors fall an hour! This is the Perseid **meteor shower**. The meteors seem to come from Perseus. This **constellation** is in the northern sky.

Perseid
meteor shower

The meteors are **debris**. They come from the **comet** Swift-Tuttle. It **orbits** the sun once every 133 years.

CHAPTER 3

Earth orbits, too. As it does, it passes through rock and dust particles left by a passing comet or **asteroid**. The particles enter our atmosphere all at once. It creates a spectacle in the night sky!

There are many shooting stars each day. If they enter into the atmosphere during the day, you might not see them. Many enter the atmosphere in other parts of the world. Look into the sky on a clear night. You could see a few shooting stars each hour! Have you ever seen a falling meteor?

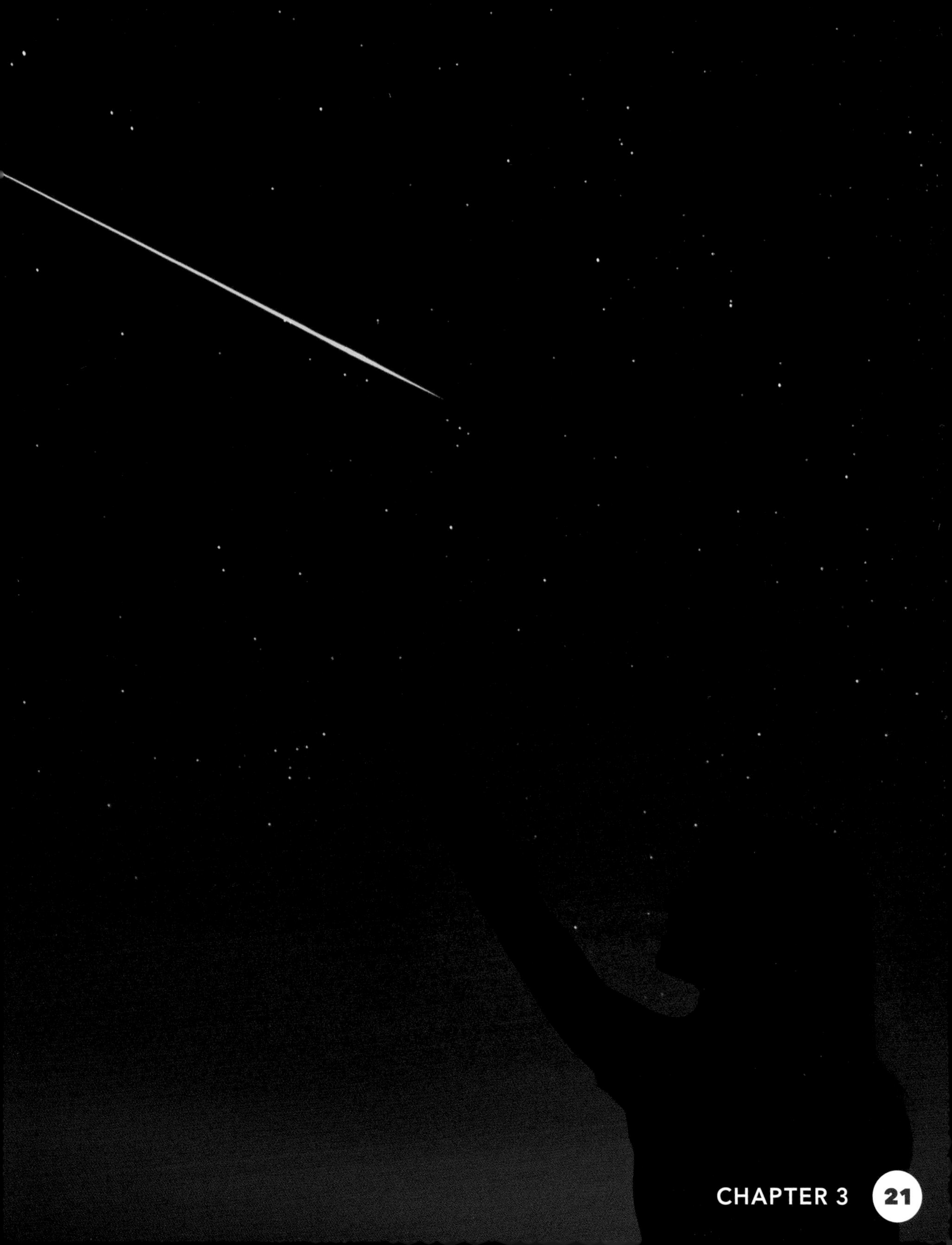

ACTIVITIES & TOOLS

THE PULL OF GRAVITY

Earth's gravity pulls objects toward the ground. Test the pull of gravity with this activity!

What You Need:
- objects of different weights, such as a feather, sheet of paper, rock, and tennis ball
- scale
- pencil and paper
- stopwatch

❶ Weigh each object on the scale. Write down each object's weight.

❷ Make a guess as to which object will fall the fastest and which will fall the slowest.

❸ Ask a friend to hold the stopwatch and time how fast it takes each object to fall to the ground.

❹ In an open area, toss each object in the air. Try to throw them the same height. Be sure to stay clear of them as they fall. Write down the time for each object.

❺ Look at your results. Which object fell the fastest? Were your guesses accurate? What does this activity tell you about gravity and the weight of objects?

GLOSSARY

asteroid: A rocky object that travels around the sun.

atmosphere: The mixture of gases that surrounds a planet or celestial body.

comet: A small chunk of dust and ice that orbits the sun.

constellation: A group of visible stars that forms a pattern when viewed from Earth.

debris: Pieces of something that has been broken or destroyed.

elements: The simple, most basic parts of something that cannot be divided into simpler substances.

friction: The force that slows down objects when they rub against each other.

gravity: The force that pulls things toward the center of Earth and keeps them from floating away.

meteorites: Meteors that survive the trip through Earth's atmosphere and hit the ground.

meteoroids: Objects in space that range in size from dust grains to small asteroids.

meteors: Pieces of rock or metal from space that speed into Earth's atmosphere and form streaks of light as they burn and fall to Earth.

meteor shower: An event during which many meteors seem to come from one point in the sky.

Northern Hemisphere: The half of Earth that is north of the equator.

orbits: Travels in a circular path around something, especially a planet or the sun.

particles: Extremely small pieces of something.

INDEX

TO LEARN MORE

Finding more information is as easy as 1, 2, 3.

❶ **Go to www.factsurfer.com**

❷ **Enter "shootingstars" into the search box.**

❸ **Click the "Surf" button to see a list of websites.**

FACT SURFER